3/18

BABY MONKEY, PRIVATE EYE

Story by Brian Selznick and David Serlin

Pictures by Brian Selznick

SCHOLASTIC PRESS · NEW YORK

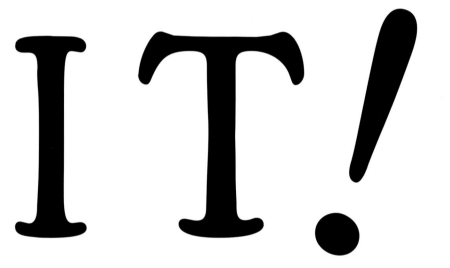

Who
is

Baby Monkey?

He is

a baby.

He is

a monkey.

He has

a job . . .

CONTENTS

CHAPTER ONE 21

CHAPTER TWO 57

CHAPTER THREE 91

CHAPTER FOUR 123

CHAPTER FIVE 163

KEY 188

INDEX 190

BIBLIOGRAPHY 191

THE CASE OF THE MISSING JEWELS!

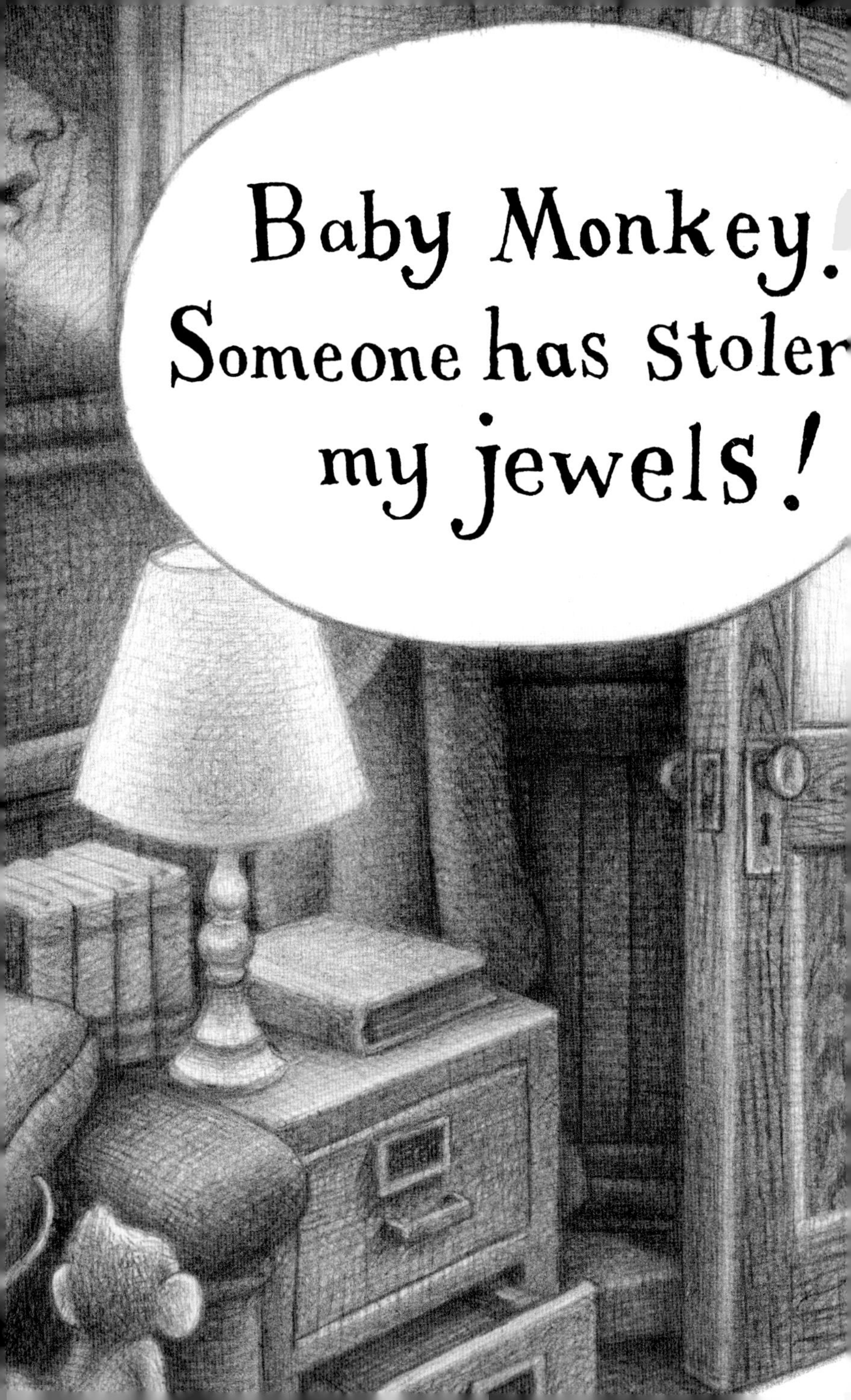
Baby Monkey.
Someone has Stolen
my jewels!

Baby Monkey can help!

Baby
Monkey
looks for
clues.

Baby Monkey writes notes.

Baby
Monkey
eats a
snack.

Baby Monkey puts on his pants.

Now
Baby
Monkey
is ready!

Baby Monkey solves the case!

Hooray
for
Baby
Monkey!

THE
CASE
OF THE
MISSING
PIZZA!

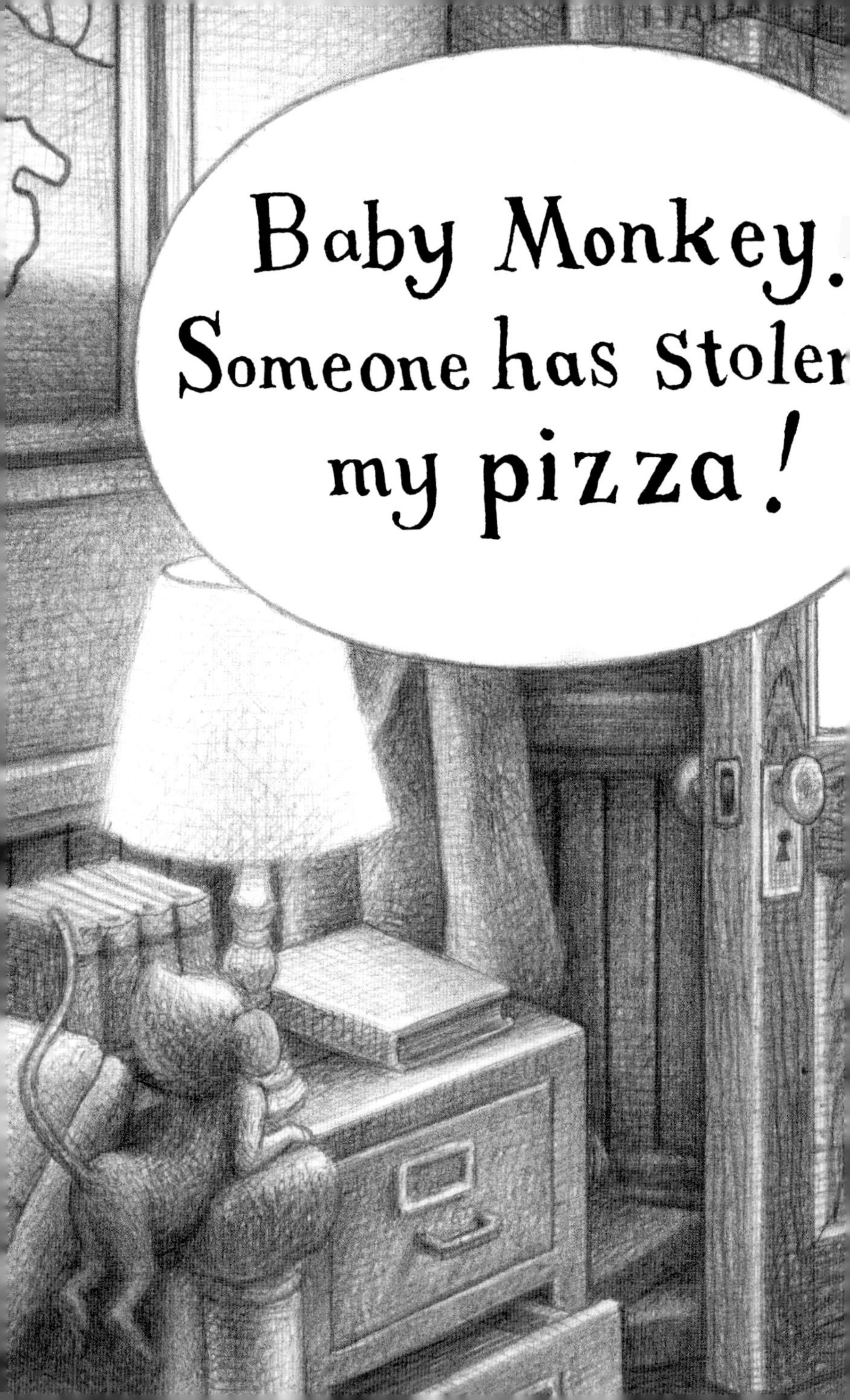
Baby Monkey.
Someone has stolen
my pizza!

Baby Monkey can help!

Baby Monkey looks for clues.

Baby Monkey writes notes.

Baby Monkey eats a snack.

Baby Monkey puts on his pants.

Now
Baby
Monkey
is ready!

Baby Monkey solves the case!

Hooray for Baby Monkey!

THE
CASE
OF THE
MISSING
NOSE*!*

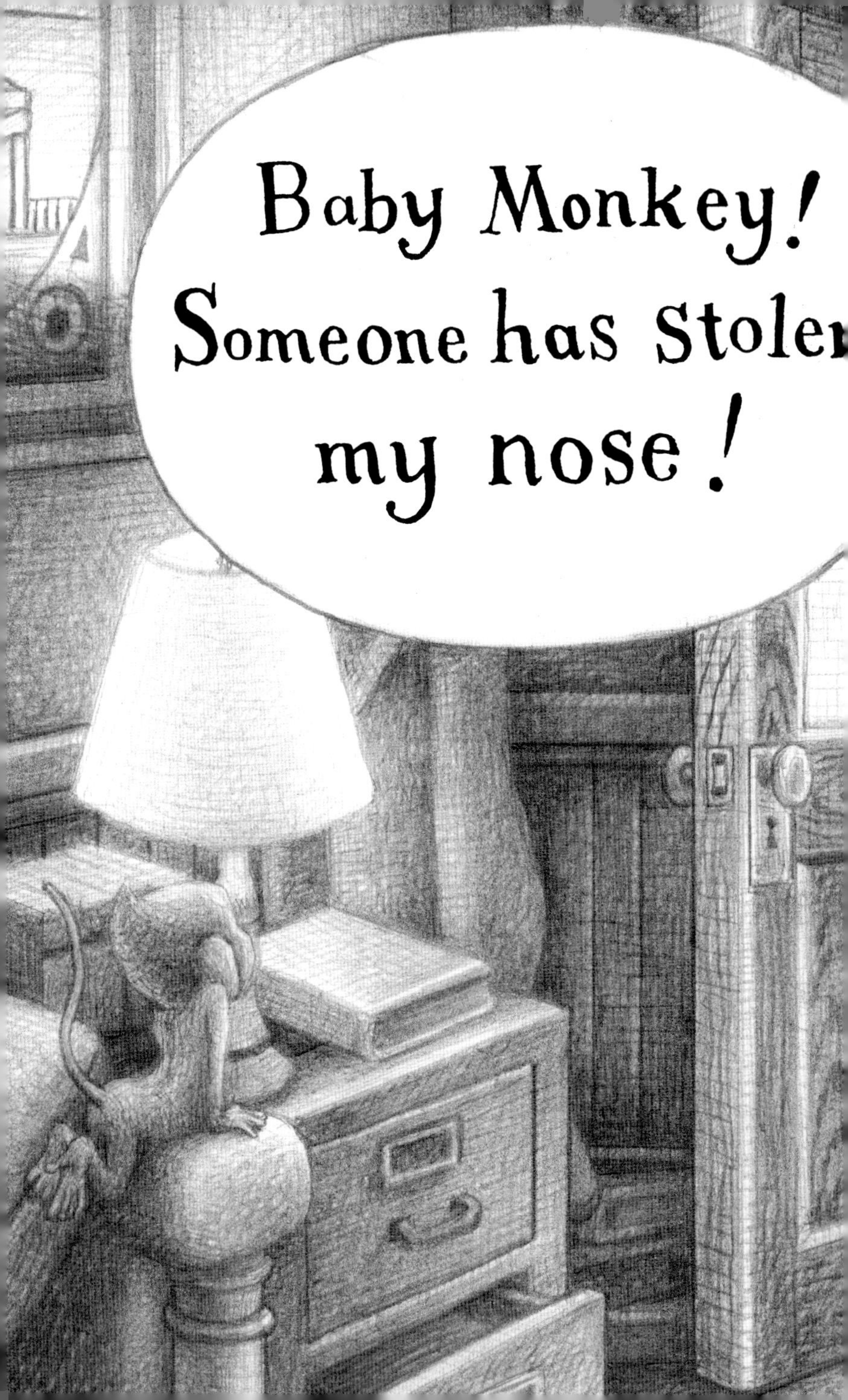
Baby Monkey! Someone has stolen my nose!

Baby Monkey can help!

Baby Monkey looks for clues.

Baby Monkey writes notes.

Baby
Monkey
eats a
snack.

Baby Monkey puts on his pants.

Now
Baby
Monkey
is ready!

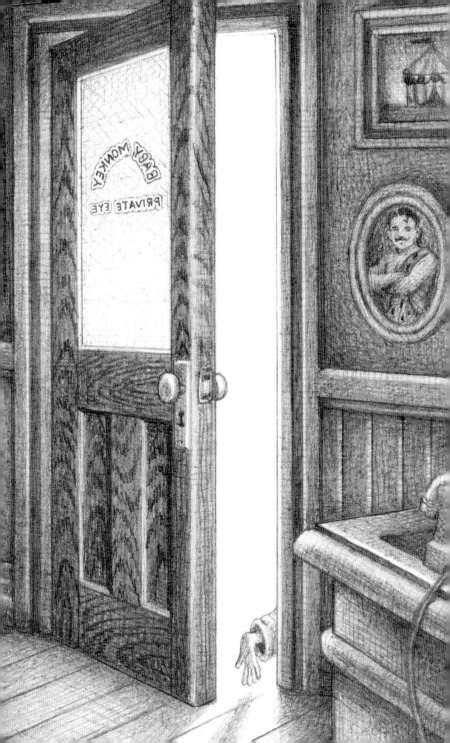

Baby Monkey solves the case!

Hooray
for
Baby
Monkey!

THE CASE OF THE MISSING SPACE- SHIP!

Baby Monkey!
Someone has Stolen
my spaceship!

Baby Monkey wants to help . . .

but . . .

Baby Monkey needs a nap.

Baby Monkey is ready.

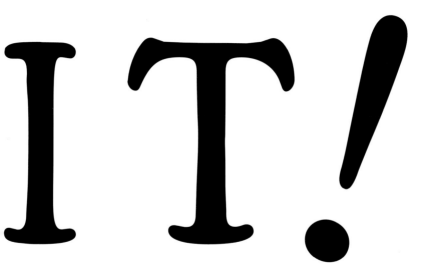

Baby
Monkey
forgot
one thing.

His
pants!

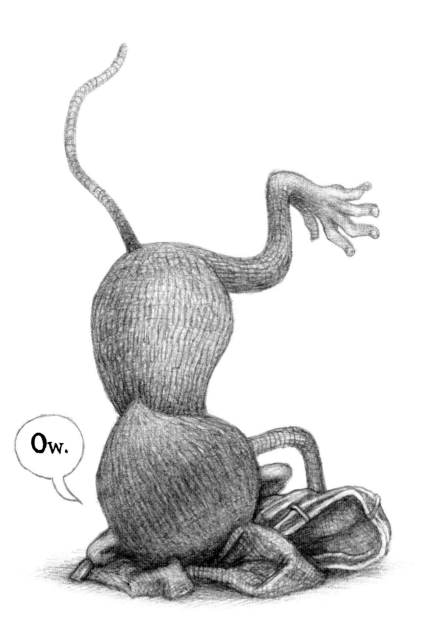

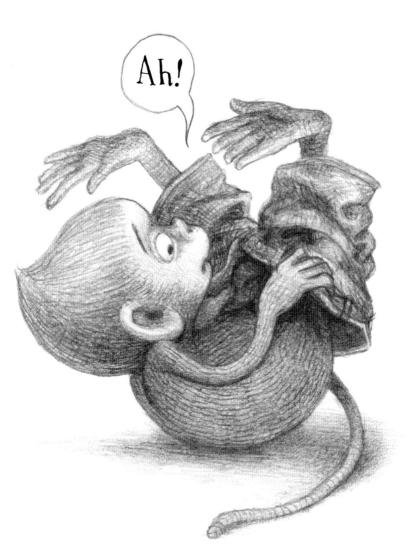

Now
Baby
Monkey
is ready!

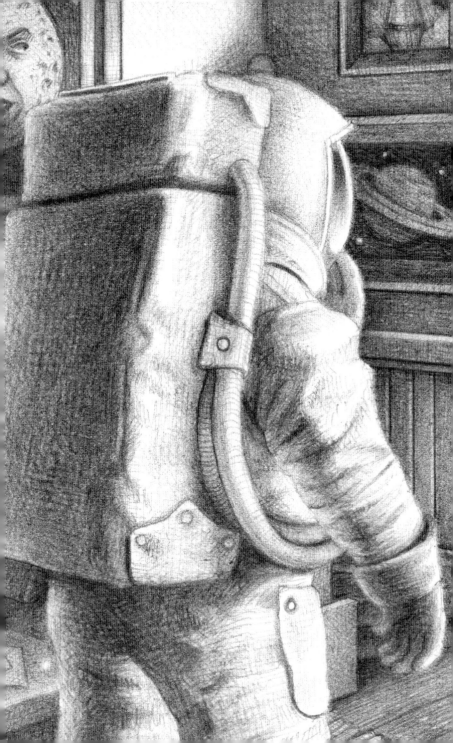

Baby Monkey solves the case!

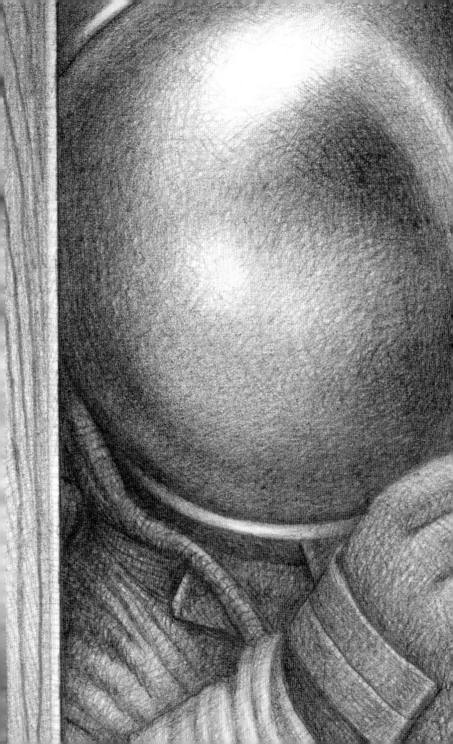

Hooray for Baby Monkey!

BABY MONKEY'S LAST CASE!

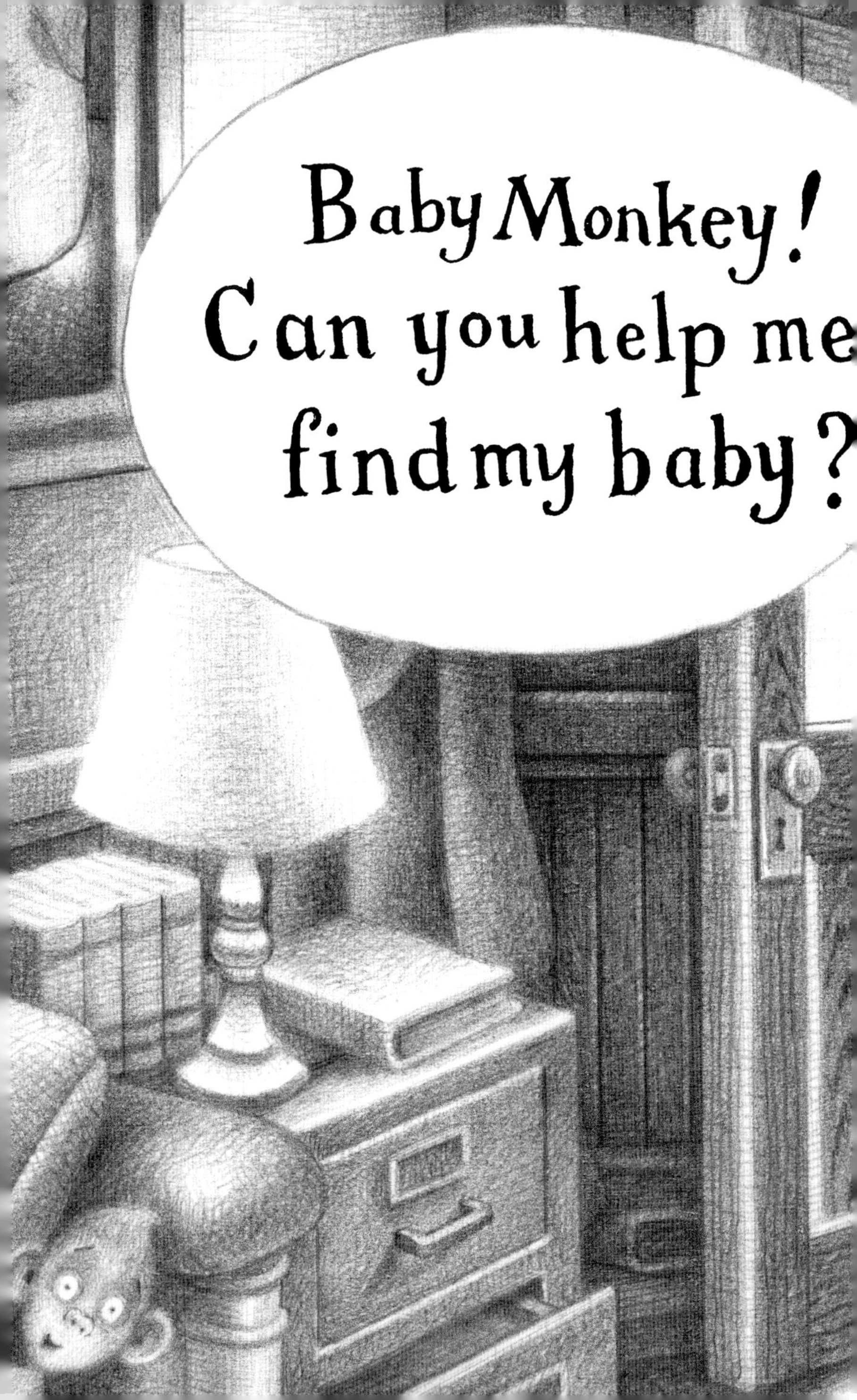
Baby Monkey! Can you help me find my baby?

YES!

No
time
for
clues.

No time for notes.

No
time
for
snacks.

No time for pants.

Baby Monkey solves the case!

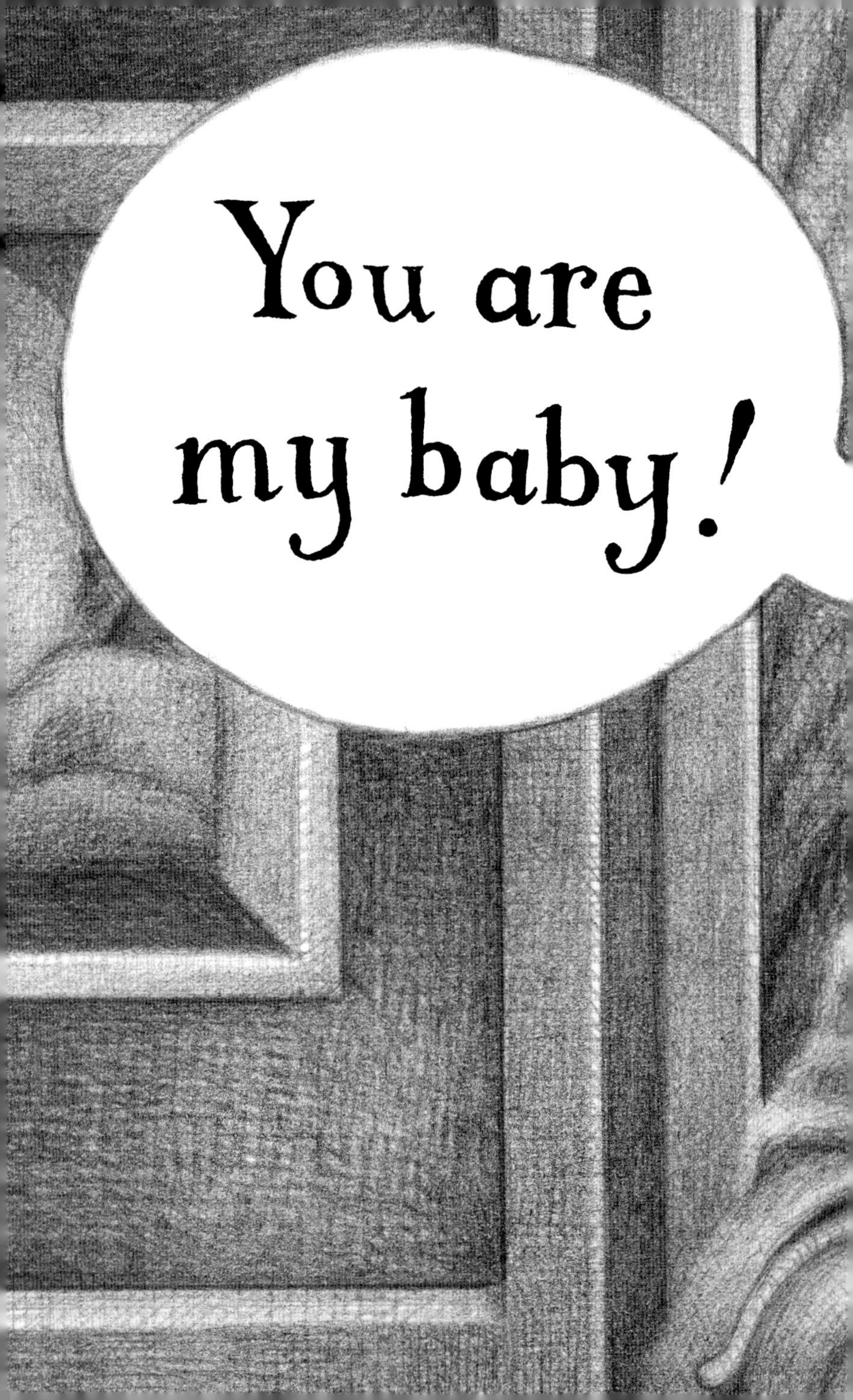
You are my baby!

Hooray
for
Baby
Monkey*!*

THE END

KEY TO
BABY MONKEY'S OFFICE

THE CASE OF THE MISSING JEWELS
(pages 22–23)

Maria Callas (1923–1977), opera singer
A Night at the Opera, 1935 Marx Brothers film
Giuseppe Verdi (1813–1901), opera composer
Palais Garnier (built 1875), the opera house of Paris
Marian Anderson (1897–1993), opera singer
Bust of Wolfgang Amadeus Mozart (1756–1791),
  composer

THE CASE OF THE MISSING PIZZA
(pages 58–59)

Map of Italy
The Italian Job, 1969 Michael Caine film
Traditional Italian restaurant setting
The Roman Colosseum, A.D. 80
Mona Lisa by Leonardo Da Vinci (1452–1519)
Bust of *David*, based on the sculpture by
  Michelangelo (1475–1564)

THE CASE OF THE MISSING NOSE
(pages 92–93)

Circus poster
Barnum, 1980 Broadway musical
Trapeze artists
Circus tent
Strong man
Bust of P.T. Barnum (1810–1891), American
  showman

THE CASE OF THE MISSING SPACESHIP
(pages 124–125)

A Trip to the Moon, 1902 Georges Méliès film
(1861–1938)

Apollo 13 blasting off (1970)

Saturn, a planet with rings

The American flag planted on the moon by Apollo 11
astronauts (1969)

Galileo Galilei, astronomer (1564–1642)

Bust of John F. Kennedy (1917–1963), American
president who helped shape the space race

BABY MONKEY'S LAST CASE
(pages 164–165)

Baby from *Madame Roulin and Her Baby*, 1888
painting by Vincent van Gogh (1853–1890)

Star Child from *2001: A Space Odyssey*, 1968 film
directed by Stanley Kubrick (1928–1999)

Baby Bonnie Blue Butler from *Gone with the Wind*,
1939 film directed by Victor Fleming (1883–1949)
and produced by David O. Selznick (1902–1965)

Mother and Child, 1905 painting by Mary Cassatt
(1844–1926)

Gerber Baby, advertising icon introduced by the
Gerber Company in 1928

Bust of Dr. Benjamin Spock (1903–1998), doctor and
baby expert

INDEX

Anderson, Marian: 23, 47

Apollo 13: 125

Apples (*see also* Snacks): 103

Astronaut: 126–127, 131, 136–137, 152, 156–157, 161

Baby, Gerber: 165

Barnum (musical): 92

Barnum, P.T.: 93, 101

Butler, Baby Bonnie Blue: 164, 181

Callas, Maria: 22, 24

Carrots, baby (*see also* Snacks): 33

Cereal (*see also* Snacks): 175

Cheese (*see also* Snacks): 134

Chef, pizza: 60, 65, 80, 84–85, 89

Clown, circus: 95, 99, 112, 116–117, 121

Coat, trench: 22–24, 58–59, 80, 92–94, 112, 125, 164–165, 180

Colosseum, the: 59, 81

Crib, baby: 186

David (Michelangelo): 59, 67

Desk: 23, 31, 47, 59, 67, 81, 93, 101, 113, 125, 133, 153, 165

Filing cabinet: 22–24, 58–59, 60, 92–94, 124–126, 164–165, 166, 180

Flag, US: 125, 153, 158, 161

Galilei, Galileo: 125, 127, 153

Hat (fedora): 23, 46, 59, 80, 93, 112, 125, 165, 180

Jewels: 53, 55

Italian Job, The (film): 59

Kennedy, John F.: 125, 133

Lamp, desk: 31, 67, 101, 133

Lion: 86–87, 186

Madame Roulin and Her Baby (Van Gogh): 164, 180

Magnifying glass: 1, 8–9, 29, 45, 48, 55, 65, 79, 82, 99, 111, 114, 131, 139, 143, 151, 154, 171

Mona Lisa (Da Vinci): 59, 61, 81

Monkey, Baby:
    and eating snacks: 32–33, 68–69, 102–103, 134, 174–175

and looking for clues: 28–29, 64–65, 98–99

and napping: 124, 132–135

and putting on pants: 34–43, 70–77, 104–109, 144–149, 177

and solving cases: 52–55, 86–89, 118–121, 158–161, 178, 183

and writing notes: 30–31, 66–67, 100–101

Monkey, Mother: 167, 181–183, 185, 186

Monkey Times: 55, 89, 121, 161

Moon, the Man in the: 124, 152

Mother and Child (Cassatt): 165

Mouse: 158, 186, 192

Mozart, W.A.: 23, 31

Needlepoint: 186

Night at the Opera, A (film): 23

Nose, red rubber: 119, 121

Peas, snap (*see also* Snacks): 69

Pizza: 86–87, 89, 192

Saturn: 125, 152

Scarf: 22, 58, 92, 124, 164, 180

Ship, space: 158–159

Singer, opera, Wagnerian: 25, 29, 46, 50, 51, 55

Snacks (*see also* Apples; Baby Carrots; Cereal; Cheese; *and* Snap Peas): 33, 69, 103, 134, 175

Snake: 118–119, 186

Spock, Benjamin: 165

Star Child: 164, 180

Strong Man: 93, 113

Telephone: 23, 31, 59, 67, 93, 101, 133, 153

Trapeze artists: 93, 112

Typewriter: 22, 58, 92, 124, 164

Verdi, Giuseppe: 23, 46

Wainscoting: 18, 22–25, 29, 31, 46–47, 58–61, 65, 67, 80–81, 92–95, 99, 101, 112–113, 124–127, 131, 133, 152–153, 164–167, 180–181, 186

Zebra: 52–53, 186

BIBLIOGRAPHY

Bathtowel, Barbara. *Famous Pizza Crimes*. Manchester, NH: Carmine Press, 1982.

Carrot, Ashley. *Animals Who Look Like They Have No Noses*. 2nd edition. Miami: Jambalaya Books, 1997.

Englehardt, Lucy. *Famous Circus Crimes*. London: Astonishing Books, 1948.

Eyelash, Melissa. *Predators Who Eat Pizza*. With an Introduction by Bartram Capshaw, Ph.D. Pittsburgh: Persephone Press, 1980.

Gergle, Luis. *Famous Jewel Crimes*. Topeka, KS: Yohé Books, 1979.

Golightly, Evan. *Pizza Pride*. Albuquerque: Harmony Press, 1992.

Hobbypocket, Herbert. *Famous Space Crimes*. East Brunswick, NJ: Irving J. Warnsdorfer, 1966.

Mobbit, Hans, and Wilma Bradenton, eds. *Tiny Animals, Giant Crimes*. Detroit: Amethyst Press, 1957.

Moshi, Moshe. *Famous Babies I Have Known*. Tel Aviv: Bubbe Books, 1988.

Pillow, Aimee. *Animals Who Like Jewelry*. Bicentennial edition. North Islip, NY: Camembert Books, 1976 [1926].

Zanzibar, Jeanine. *Healthy Snacks for Growing Primates*. Madison, WI: Harlow Books, 1994.

Text copyright © 2018 by Brian Selznick and David Serlin

Illustrations copyright © 2018 by Brian Selznick

Library of Congress Cataloging-in-Publication Data available

ISBN 978-1-338-18061-9   10 9 8 7 6 5 4 3 2 1   18 19 20 21 22

Printed in China 38   First edition, March 2018

The text of this book was set in Cooper Oldstyle Light. The display type and word balloons were hand-lettered by Brian Selznick. The drawings were created in pencil on Arches watercolor paper. The book was printed on 170 GSM LumiSilk Matte Art Paper and was thread-sewn in 16-page signatures by King Yip (Dongguan) Printing & Packaging Co., Ltd., China. Production was overseen by Angie Chen. Manufacturing was supervised by Irene Chan. The book was designed by Brian Selznick, Charles Kreloff, and David Saylor, and edited by Tracy Mack.

This book is dedicated to our mothers,

Lynn Selznick and Renee Serlin.